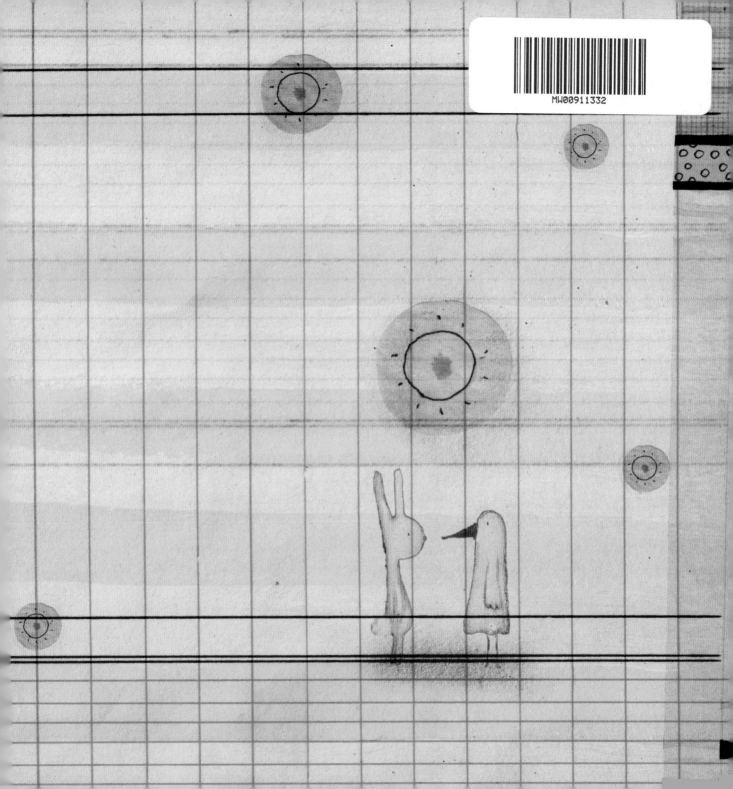

Original edition, entitled *Cerca*, copyright © 2008 by Kalandraka Editoria
Text and illustrations copyright © Natalia Colombo, 2008

English translation published by Tundra Books, 2010

Published in Canada by Tundra Books,
75 Sherbourne Street, Toronto, Ontario M5A 2P9

Published in the United States by Tundra Books of Northern New York,
P.O. Box 1030, Plattsburgh, New York 12901

Library of Congress Control Number: 2009941816

Library and Archives Canada Cataloguing in Publication
Colombo, Natalia
So close / Natalia Colombo.

Translation of: Cerca.
Interest age level: For ages 4-7.
ISBN 978-1-77049-207-3

I. Title.

PZ10.3.C65So 2010   j863   C2009-905381-0

We acknowledge the financial support of the Government of Canada through the Book Publishing Industry Development Program (BPIDP)
and that of the Government of Ontario through the Ontario Media Development Corporation's Ontario Book Initiative.
We further acknowledge the support of the Canada Council for the Arts and the Ontario Arts Council for our publishing program.

ONTARIO ARTS COUNCIL
CONSEIL DES ARTS DE L'ONTARIO

Printed and bound in China

1 2 3 4 5 6   15 14 13 12 11 10

NATALIA COLOMBO

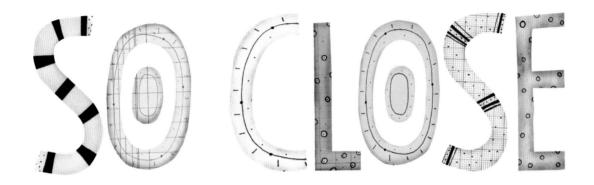

SO CLOSE

TUNDRA BOOKS

MR. DUCK
IS GOING TO WORK,
LIKE HE DOES EVERY DAY.

MR. RABBIT
IS ALSO GOING TO WORK,
LIKE HE DOES EVERY DAY.

THEY ALWAYS WALK
PAST EACH OTHER.

ON THE WAY
TO WORK...

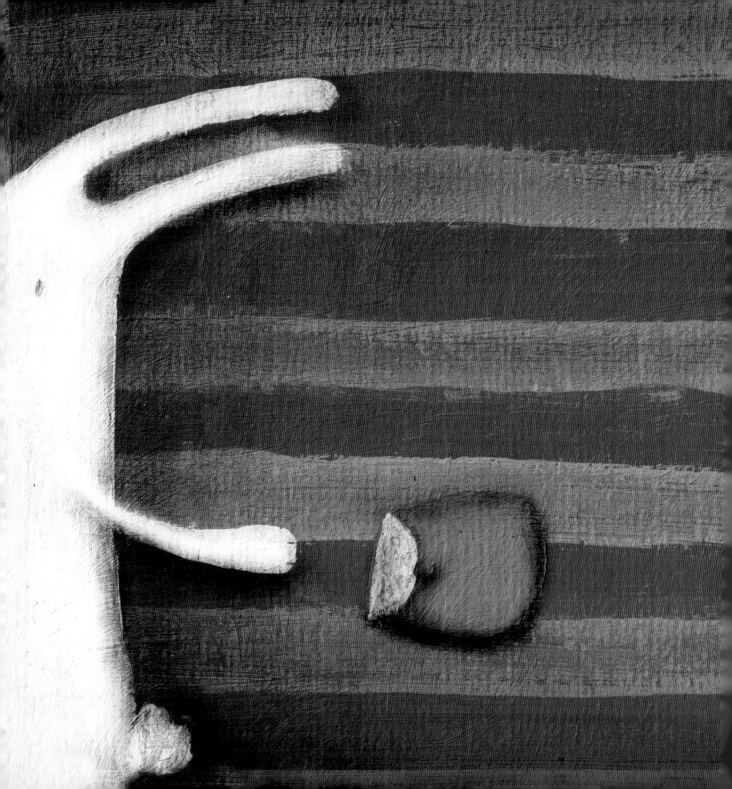

WHETHER THEY'RE SAD

OR HA Y...

IN THEIR CARS...

OR OUT
ON THEIR BIKES.

THEY NEVER SAY HELLO.

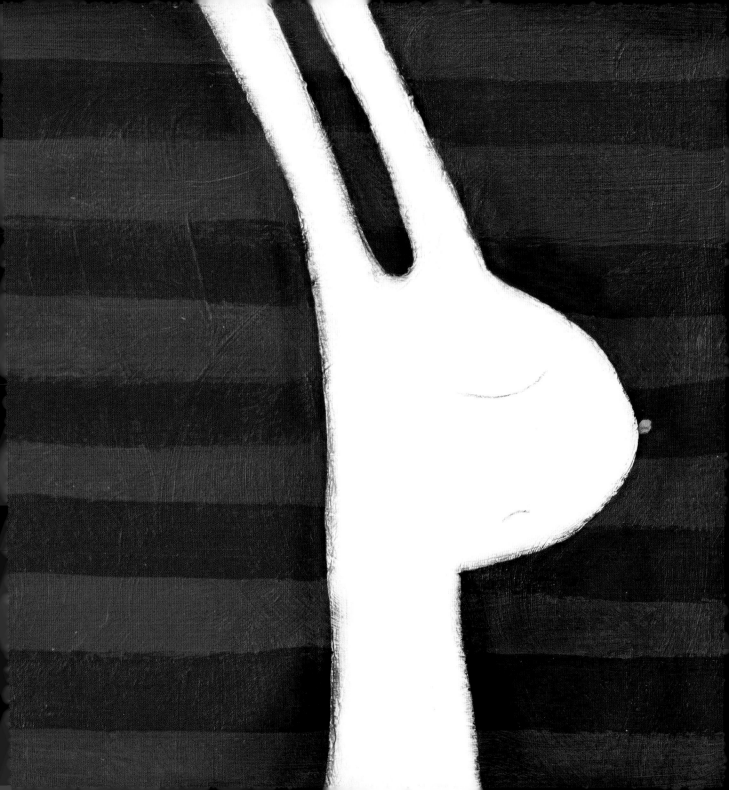

WHAT A

DIFFERENCE...

ONE LITTLE WORD

COULD MAKE.

HELLO

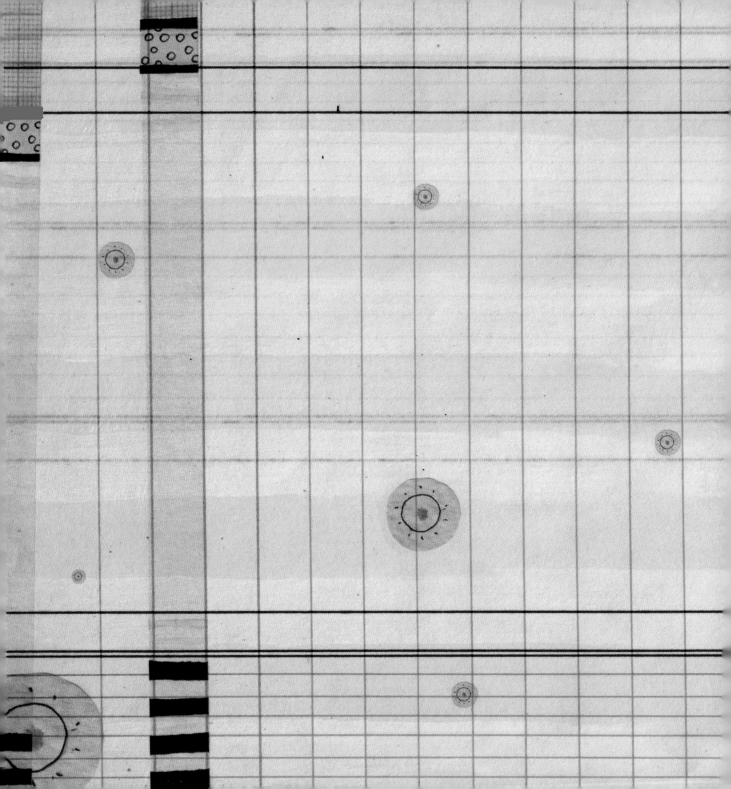